The Foundling

Clarion Books
a Houghton Mifflin Company imprint
215 Park Avenue South, New York, NY 10003
Text copyright © 1977 by Carol Carrick
Illustrations copyright © 1977 by Donald Carrick
All rights reserved.
For information about permission to reproduce
selections from this book, write to Permissions,
Houghton Mifflin Company, 2 Park Street, Boston, MA 02108
Printed in the USA

Library of Congress Cataloging in Publication Data

Carrick, Carol.   The foundling.
Summary: memories of his dog, killed in an accident, cause
Christopher to resist his parents' efforts to adopt a puppy.
[1. Dogs—Fiction] I. Carrick, Donald. II. Title.
PZ7.C2344Fo   [E]   77-1587
ISBN 0-395-28775-8   PA 0-89919-466-4
(Previously published by The Seabury
Press under ISBN 0-8164-3199-X)
HOR 10 9 8

The Foundling

by CAROL CARRICK

pictures by DONALD CARRICK

Clarion Books / New York

The Tilton family next door to Christopher had a new dog... still a puppy, really. He had come through the gate one day when Christopher got home from school.

Christopher sat down next to the puppy and scratched his head. Except for the rings around his eyes and his dark ears, he looked the way Christopher's dog, Bodger, must have looked when he was a puppy. Christopher didn't remember because he had been a baby then himself.

The puppy sniffed at Christopher's lunch box, trying to nuzzle it open. Christopher fed him the scrap of uneaten sandwich inside. After that, the puppy waited for him every day after school.

Even though Bodger had been killed by a pickup truck, Christopher found himself hoping every night that his bedroom door would be shoved open and Bodger's warm weight would settle on his feet. The bad dreams that came for weeks after the accident had stopped, and Christopher didn't lie awake any more, reliving the accident. But it was hard getting used to Bodger being gone.

Maybe it was seeing Christopher play all week with the little dog from next door that gave his father the idea. On Saturday, when Christopher was bouncing a ball off the roof of the porch, his father came out and nodded toward the car.

"Hop in. I've got a surprise for you."

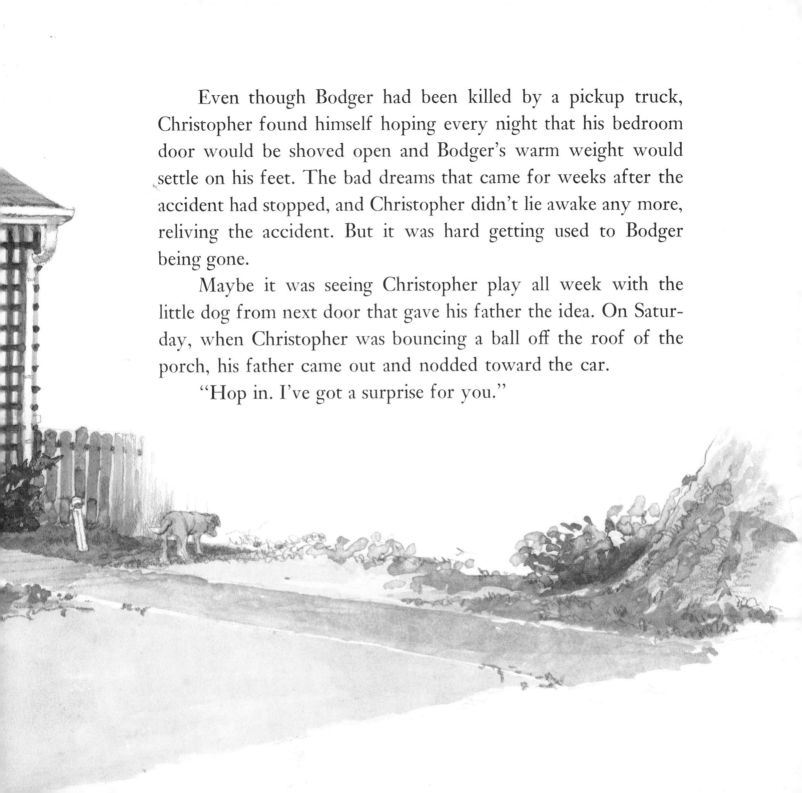

Christopher felt excited and wondered what the surprise could be. But when they stopped in front of a small building with a sign out front that said "ANIMAL SHELTER," his head snapped toward his father in panic.

"We're going to get a dog," he said. "Dad, I don't want another one."

His father put a hand on Christopher's shoulder. "Just come in with me. It can't hurt to look. Can it?"

"Please, Dad. There won't ever be another dog like Bodger."

"I know," his father said very quietly.

For the first time Christopher realized that his father missed Bodger, too.

After ringing a bell, they went inside to a waiting room. A man in a white coat came through an inner door.

"This is Christopher," his father said. "Christopher, I want you to meet Dr. Walker."

"I hear you like dogs, Chris," the doctor said with a friendly smile.

Christopher knew his father would be angry with him if he was rude, so he gave the man a half smile. Then he put his hands in his pockets and stared again at the floor.

The doctor held open the inner door that led to a long white room with a cement floor and tile walls. At either end, dogs were in cells like a jail. There was a table and sink to one side. Everything was very clean.

"Why aren't they making any noise?" Christopher asked.

"Most of these animals are sick," the doctor explained. "They get plenty noisy when they're ready to go home. Here's the fellow who would like to meet you."

When they stopped in front of a row of small cages, a spotted puppy stood up on his hind legs. He shoved his gumdrop nose between the bars and wagged his tail furiously.

"Boy, he's a lively one." Christopher's father laughed. "He really wants to get out of there."

"Mmm," answered Christopher without much enthusiasm.

The doctor opened the cage door and lifted out the puppy. "Here. Would you like to hold him?" he asked.

Christopher only shrugged in reply, but he took the puppy anyway.

"After vacation time we get a lot of cats and dogs that people abandon when they go back to the city," the doctor said. "If they weren't brought here, most of these animals would get sick or starve."

Christopher held the puppy to his face. It felt silky and warm. He could hear how fast its heart was beating.

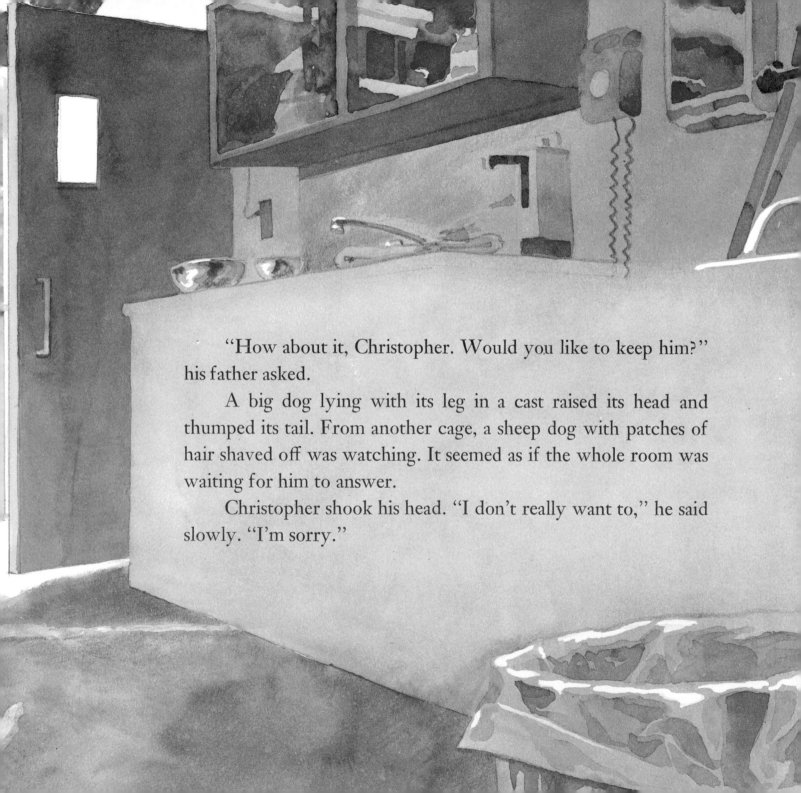

"How about it, Christopher. Would you like to keep him?" his father asked.

A big dog lying with its leg in a cast raised its head and thumped its tail. From another cage, a sheep dog with patches of hair shaved off was watching. It seemed as if the whole room was waiting for him to answer.

Christopher shook his head. "I don't really want to," he said slowly. "I'm sorry."

When Christopher got in the car he wasn't so sure that he had made the right decision. The trip home seemed to take forever. Neither he nor his father said anything. Christopher knew he ought to explain why he didn't want the puppy except he didn't exactly know himself. He only knew how he felt. But he did feel guilty about the puppy in the cage.

"Dad, if we don't take the puppy, do you think someone else will?"

"They might."

"Don't you think it would be unfaithful to Bodger to get another dog . . . right away, I mean?"

"Christopher, it might be a good way to show that you loved having Bodger—if you rescued another little dog and took care of him."

"Well, I don't want another dog. At least not that dog. I don't want just any dog."

As the car pulled up in the driveway, Christopher's mother came out of the house. "Where's the puppy?" she asked. "I can't wait to see him."

She looked at Christopher's face, then at his father's. "What's the matter? What's happened?"

Christopher picked up his bike from where it had been left on the lawn.

"Look, I don't want another dog," he said. "Do I have to take one just because no one else wants it? Why don't you leave me alone." And he pedaled off.

After he had gotten away from the house, Christopher cruised around, thinking. Would he have chosen Bodger the first time he saw him? he wondered. Bodger had always just been there, like his parents. He loved them without thinking about it. Now they were only trying to help him, and he'd let them down. Maybe he should go home and tell them he would take the puppy after all.

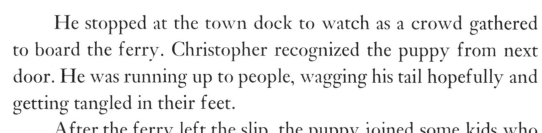

He stopped at the town dock to watch as a crowd gathered to board the ferry. Christopher recognized the puppy from next door. He was running up to people, wagging his tail hopefully and getting tangled in their feet.

After the ferry left the slip, the puppy joined some kids who were fishing. He sniffed a landed snapper and then jumped back, startled, when the fish flapped on the dock. The boys laughed as the puppy regained enough courage to bark at the fish. But when he knocked over their bait pail, they chased him off.

Christopher picked up the puppy.

"You're pretty far from home. You'd better come back with me."

He wrapped the puppy in his jacket and stuffed him in the bicycle basket. On the way back the puppy wriggled free enough to poke out his head. His ears had flopped inside out.

"You really are cute," Christopher said. "You look like my old panda bear. His name was Ben."

When they got home Christopher brought the puppy to the back of the house next door.

"Here's your dog, Mrs. Tilton. I found him on the dock. He was lost." Christopher felt quite proud of himself.

"*My* dog? That's not *my* dog," said Mrs. Tilton. "No sir! I wouldn't even let it in the house. My husband says, 'Give the poor thing something to eat. It's starving.' Oh no. You give these stray animals food and that's it. You can't get rid of them for any- thing. . . ."

Christopher scooped up the puppy who had been pulling the laces from his shoe. A wonderful idea swelled inside him until a grin spread across his face. As he left Mrs. Tilton's yard her voice continued from somewhere between the sheets she was taking down.

"It's these summer people. They can't resist getting a cute little puppy. Then, when it comes time to go home, they just dump it and expect other people to take care of it. Well, not me. . . ."

Her voice was cut off as the back door banged shut behind Christopher. His parents had already started lunch.

"Hey Mom," Christopher said, "do we have something I can give Ben to eat? He's really starved."

"You shouldn't feed the Tiltons' dog," she said. "He already has a home."

"No, Mom. That's just it. He doesn't belong to *anyone*."

Christopher opened the refrigerator door. With Ben wriggling under one arm, he rummaged through the shelves looking for something a puppy might eat—his puppy.